DATE DUE

Demco, Inc. 38-293

CLAUDIA
CRISTINA CORTEZ
UNCOMPLICATES YOUR LIFE

Advice
ABOUT FAMILY
BY DIANA G. GALLAGHER

ILLUSTRATED BY BRANN GARVEY

McLean County Unit #5
201-EJHS

STONE ARCH BOOKS
a capstone imprint

Claudia Cristina Cortez are published by Stone Arch Books
A Capstone Imprint
151 Good Counsel Drive, P.O. Box 669
Mankato, Minnesota 56002
www.capstonepub.com

Printed in the United States of America in Stevens Point, Wisconsin.
092009
005619WZS10

Library of Congress Cataloging-in-Publication Data
Gallagher, Diana G.
  Advice about family: Claudia Cristina Cortez uncomplicates your life/
  by Diana G. Gallagher; illustrated by Brann Garvey.
  p. cm. — (Claudia Cristina Cortez)
  ISBN 978-1-4342-1907-7 (library binding)
  ISBN 978-1-4342-2250-3 (paperback)
  1. Families—Juvenile literature. 2. Interpersonal relations—Juvenile literature.
I. Garvey, Brann. II. Title
  HQ744.G415 2010
  306.85—dc22   2009034682

ART DIRECTOR/GRAPHIC DESIGNER: *Kay Fraser*
PRODUCTION SPECIALIST: *Michelle Biedscheid*
PHOTO CREDITS: *Delaney Photography*

CLAUDIA

CAST OF

ME

CLAUDIA

That's me. I'm thirteen, and I'm in the seventh grade at Pine Tree Middle School. I live with my mom, my dad, and my brother, Jimmy. I have one cat, Ping-Ping. I like music, baseball, and hanging out with my friends.

MONICA is my very best friend. We met when we were really little, and we've been best friends ever since. I don't know what I'd do without her! Monica loves horses. In fact, when she grows up, she wants to be an Olympic rider!

MONICA

BECCA

BECCA is one of my closest friends. She lives next door to Monica. Becca is really, really smart. She gets good grades. She's also really good at art.

CHARACTERS

TOMMY's our class clown. Sometimes he's really funny, but sometimes he is just annoying. Becca has a crush on him . . . but I'd never tell.

TOMMY

PETER

I think **PETER** is probably the smartest person I've ever met. Seriously. He's even smarter than our teachers! He's also one of my friends. Which is lucky, because sometimes he helps me with homework.

ADAM and I met when we were in third grade. Now that we're teenagers, we don't spend as much time together as we did when we were kids, but he's always there for me when I need him. (Plus, he's the only person who wants to talk about baseball with me!)

ADAM

CAST OF

ANGELA is Monica's eight-year-old stepsister. Monica says that it hasn't been easy having a little stepsister. But since it is important to her mom, she has figured out lots of ways to be a good big sister.

ANGELA

AUNT INEZ is my mom's sister, so she is my aunt. She is also my cousin Laura's mom. She makes really delicious meals — I think she is the best cook I know!

AUNT INEZ

LAURA is my oldest — and favorite — cousin. I have always looked up to Laura, and I sort of think of her as the older sister I never had. She's pretty, smart, funny, and a great cousin!

LAURA

CHARACTERS

ALISHA is my seven-year-old cousin. I used to think she was always crabby and never smiled. It seemed like her favorite thing to do was complain. But I think I figured her out. Even though I don't see her a lot, I have fun with her when I do!

ALISHA

JOSE

JOSE is Alisha's six-year-old brother. He likes watching TV. He is also obsessed with pirates. If Jose isn't watching cartoons, he is trying to figure out a way to watch cartoons.

GABE is Alisha and Jose's three-year-old brother. Sometimes it seems like the only thing Gabe likes to do is cry. He's pretty cute, but he's always getting into my stuff and wrecking things.

GABE

INTRODUCTION

When you're thirteen years old, like I am, you're *stuck with your family*. Luckily, I like my family. A lot! But I know some kids don't like their families as much as I do.

That can be hard when you have to spend so much time with your family members. After all, we won't get our **DRIVERS' LICENSES** for at least three more years. Until then, we have to rely on our parents for everything. (I am saving up money so that I can buy a car the second I turn 16!)

NOTE: All families are DIFFERENT. Even in my group of friends, no two families are exactly the same. (You can read all about different types of families on page 12.) So in this book, when I talk about my family, it doesn't mean that your family is **weird** if it's different. It's not. Unless all families are weird (which, maybe, they are!).

▷ CHAPTER 1
FAMILY BASICS:
What makes a family a family

Before we get too **deep** into my advice on family, you should know who I'm talking about. These are the **MAIN MEMBERS** of my family:

JIMMY

My big brother loves playing music in his band. He is *obsessed* with computers and computer games. He and I don't always get along. He's always kicking me out of his room. And I'm always *annoying* him. But sometimes we are good friends.

MOM

Mom reminds me to eat my vegetables, clean my room, and help with the **laundry**. She likes *volunteering* at the Humane Society and going for walks with her friends. I go to her for advice sometimes. But I never talk to her about boys!

DAD

Dad owns **cortez computers**, a computer store in my town. He is very serious and busy. Sometimes I feel like he doesn't understand me. But I know he always loves me.

PING-PING

My Siamese cat is the only *non-human* member of the family. She's also the best listener, and she **sleeps** the most.

UNCLE DIEGO

I have other aunts and uncles, but Uncle Diego is the one I know the *best*. He lives in the same town as us. So he spends a lot of time at our house. Uncle Diego isn't like other adults I know. He treats me like an **EQUAL**, and he loves having fun.

GRANDMA

Grandma lives nearby, and sometimes she stays at our house. I love having Grandma around. We *read books* together, talk for hours, and **pig out** on ice cream. She's a great cook, and I trust her.

And then there's me, Claudia!

DIFFERENT KINDS OF FAMILIES

Quiz: Which one is the REAL FAMILY?

1. Mom, Dad, brothers and sisters, you

2. Mom, Grandpa, sister, you

3. Dad, stepmother, stepbrother, you

4. Grandma, you

Answer: All of the above!

I live in a house with *two parents* and my BROTHER. But not all families are like that.

Some kids are raised by their **grandparents.**

Some live with just ONE parent.

Some live with one parent and a **stepparent**, or even **divide** their time between two houses.

There's no one right way for a family to be. Having different kinds of people is just another thing that keeps families interesting.

My Family, by Monica

Monica stepping in here to tell you a little about my family. My dad died when I was little. A few years later, my mom *remarried*. My new stepdad and his daughter, Angela, moved into our house. Angela is eight.

It hasn't been easy having a *stepsister*. I like Angela. But sometimes she really gets on my nerves. She always **bugs** me and my friends when we're trying to hang out in peace and quiet. **That's really annoying.**

My mom says I should include her. But that's hard to do, since she doesn't exactly want to do the same kinds of things we do.

After all, she still thinks boys are *gross*, and we don't! And she barely knows how to tie her shoes, let alone go shopping for clothes.

But that didn't matter to my mom. She said I had to *work* to find ways to spend time with Angela. Otherwise, we'd never get along.

So I came up with some ideas.

Here are some things that ARE fun to do with younger siblings, stepsiblings, cousins, or other younger kids.

- Go to a *toy store*. It's a fun excuse to go to the store. After all, without your younger sibling, you might feel like you're too old to hang out there. But it's still a fun place to go.

- Go out for ice cream, or have a **sundae night** at your house.

- Play kiddie games with them, like **hide-and-seek,** tag, or house.

- Watch their favorite movie or play 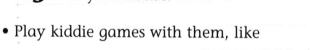 their favorite **video game**.

- Play **cards**. Let them win sometimes!

- Give them *attention*. I've learned from being Angela's big sister for three years that little siblings think their older siblings are **really cool.** They just want attention from us.

My stepdad wasn't as easy to deal with. I have always liked him. But it was *hard* for me, at first, to have another adult living in my house. I was used to it just being **me and Mom**. I didn't want to follow my stepdad's rules. I didn't think he should be allowed to **boss me around.**

Then I found out that we both love *dance competitions* on TV. It's kind of a funny thing for a dad to like, right? But he does. He gets really into the shows. He yells at the judges, and he always picks the WINNER during the second episode.

We started watching them together. Pretty soon, we were having a good time while we watched. And before I knew it, I felt like he was part of my family. Not my dad, but **not just some guy** who was married to my mom, either.

It took work for both of us. I had to ACCEPT that he and my mom loved each other and were going to stay married. My stepdad had to accept that I had spent ten years without him living in our house. So it would take time for me to think of him as a member of my family. Now we're **ONE BIG HAPPY FAMILY**.

– Monica

▷CHAPTER 2
PONDERING PARENTS:
The good, the bad, & the public

My parents know me better than anyone else. They were there when I was born. And they've been around me for my whole life.

I've learned more from my parents than I've learned from all of my teachers combined.

Lots of times, I really *love* being with my parents.

My mom is really **SMART** and has a lot of the same hobbies that I have.

We both love reading and baking cupcakes. Neither of us likes **CAULIFLOWER** or super sappy movies.

My dad is more **serious** than I am. But we both love action movies and watching baseball on TV. However, neither of us likes *runny eggs* or staying inside on sunny days.

What about your parents? How are you the same? How are you different? If you have siblings, how are they like or unlike your parents?

PARENTS

. . . want to help you **grow** and *learn*.

. . . treat you like a little kid, even though you're NOT.

. . . can help solve fights between you and your siblings.

. . . are sometimes really *embarrassing*.

. . . know lots of old jokes.

. . . always want to know **everything** about your life (even when you **REALLY** don't want to tell them).

. . . remember funny stories about your childhood (and sometimes have the photos to prove it).

. . . boss you around.

. . . LOVE you for who you are.

. . . can be **frustrating**.

. . . can be a lot of **fun**.

. . . *love you no matter what!*

Something **weird** happens when you're my age. All of a sudden, your parents become SUPER EMBARRASSING. I don't know how it happens or why. But it's like one day, your parents are pretty cool and fun. The next, they are *mortifying*.

Jimmy says the same thing happened to him when he was my age. All of a sudden, he noticed that Mom and Dad wore **dorky clothes.** They didn't know cool slang. They listened to **terrible music.** And they were embarrassing to be around outside of our house.

The same thing is happening to my friends. All of them report that their parents have suddenly become horribly embarrassing.

So what's a normal thirteen-year-old to do?

I asked Jimmy and my friends to help me come up with a list of *ways to deal* with our embarrassing parents.

I asked: **"What do you do when your parents are embarrassing you in front of other people?"**

ADAM said, "I ignore it. My parents aren't trying to embarrass me on purpose, so I just pretend it isn't happening."

Monica said, "I try to **stay calm**. Freaking out about my stepdad's habit of wearing long socks with sandals isn't going to make him stop doing it. If I stay calm, I don't get as worried about it."

Becca said, "My mom does this thing where we'll be at the grocery store and a song will come on and she sings along. So I started getting back at her by singing along. Only I sing **REALLY LOUD AND OFF-KEY**. I think she got the point, because she stopped doing it."

JIMMY said, "When Mom and Dad embarrass me in public, I just try to **walk behind them** a few steps. That way, no one knows we're together."

Tommy said, "I just make **jokes** about it to whoever is there. That way I don't feel embarrassed."

I hope one of these tricks works for me!

FIGHTING WITH PARENTS

I think every thirteen-year-old girl must **get in trouble** sometimes. It is impossible to never fight with your parents. My aunt Inez says that when she and Mom were my age, they fought with my grandma and grandpa *all the time.*

But that doesn't make it easy. Fighting with your parents is hard for you and for them. **Nobody likes arguing**, especially with people in their family.

Unfortunately, the teenage years are hard for kids. My mom says it is hard for the parents too. I **HATE** fighting with my mom and dad, but it still happens.

Sometimes it happens because I don't do something they want me to do. Sometimes it happens because *they don't listen to me,* or they're not being fair. Sometimes it happens for no reason at all — it just happens.

My friends say that fights happen in their houses for the same reasons.

If you find yourself in a fight with your parents, try these tips:

- Take a *deep breath*.

- Give yourself a break. **Leave the room** to calm down. It might not happen right away. It might even take a day or two to calm down.

- Try to see the argument from their point of view. Why are they upset? **HOW WOULD YOU FEEL** if you were them?

- Be **HONEST**. Explain how you're feeling and why.

- Use a *calm voice*. If you're calm, everyone else will calm down too.

- Think creatively. **Work together**. How can you end the argument?

- If you're wrong, **APOLOGIZE** — and mean it. Don't apologize until you're ready. And remember, an apology doesn't mean anything unless you mean it!

- Never let an argument fester for long. *Solve it fast*. And try to not let the same argument happen again.

▷ CHAPTER 3
SIBLING SCENE:
The pros & cons of sharing parents

Siblings . . .

. . . might *tattle* on you, if you are fighting.

. . . are good for **pillow fights** and watching movies on rainy days.

. . . can be really annoying.

. . . **stick up for you** when someone puts you down.

. . . argue with you over what to watch on TV or what video game to play.

. . . aren't always so bad!

I have one brother, Jimmy. When I was little, I used to wish Jimmy was a girl. I thought it would be so great to have someone to **PLAY DOLLS** with and maybe share clothes with.

I could tell her all my SECRETS, and she could tell me hers. Every night would feel like a sleepover because we would be such good friends.

Now that I'm older, I know that even if Jimmy were a girl, we would still probably ANNOY each other sometimes. I probably wouldn't want to share all my clothes. I might not want to tell my secrets to a family member, even to a sister. And even though he's a boy, Jimmy is still a **good friend**.

It is nice to have siblings, because they are the only ones who know what it's like to deal with your particular set of parents. They probably have to follow the same RULES. (If they are older than you, their rules might not be as strict now. But they probably were when they were your age.)

Siblings will **understand** if your parents are being unreasonable. They might even be able to talk to your parents for you.

But sometimes siblings can *get on your nerves*. Maybe your brother gets all of the attention. Maybe your sister always comes barging into your room **WITHOUT KNOCKING**. You just need to figure out ways to put up with them. Don't let arguments get out of hand. REMEMBER: there are a lot of pros to having siblings.

Sometimes I think I'd rather be an only child than have a *big brother*. I love my brother, but we don't always get along. But then, just when he's annoyed me so much I'm ready to sell him to my neighbors, he'll do something really NICE, and I change my mind.

Since I became a teenager, Jimmy has gotten more helpful. Even so, I don't go to Jimmy for help with all of my problems. For instance, I don't think he'd really be able to help much when I'm having **boy problems** or fighting with one of my best friends.

Big brothers (or sisters, too) are good for some things, like . . .

. . . **helping with computer problems.** Jimmy knows everything about computers, and he always fixes mine whenever something goes wrong.

. . . **playing video games.** Jimmy teaches me all the secret cheats and codes.

. . . *studying for tests.* Jimmy already took the same classes when he was in seventh grade, so he can help me out.

. . . driving you to school or to the mall. Jimmy recently got his driver's license, so he'll take any chance he can to give me a ride because it means he gets to drive!

. . . COVERING FOR YOU TO MAKE SURE YOU STAY OUT OF TROUBLE. Jimmy helps me stay out of trouble, and I help him.

. . . helping out with school projects by doing things like donating stuff for your school rummage sale. Every year, the seventh grade has a big rummage sale. I donated some pony dolls to Jimmy's sale, and he donated some trading cards to mine. And when we had to sell candy, he bought six chocolate bars!

. . . giving advice about how to deal with your parents. Jimmy has known my parents longer than I have, so he knows what he's talking about!

I guess having a big brother isn't so bad after all. But I'll never tell Jimmy that!

1. While your parents are at work, you and your brother are supposed to **clean the house.** Instead of helping, he's playing video games. How do you react?

   a. You just do it all yourself. There's *no point* in starting a fight.

   b. You POLITELY remind him that he's supposed to help.

   c. You **scream** at him and refuse to work alone.

2. Your sister *barges* into your room without knocking. What do you do?

   a. Nothing. What's the point?

   b. Tell her that if she wants to come in, she needs to KNOCK. Then ask her to go and try again.

   c. **Scream** and threaten to hit her.

3. Your siblings want to order **pizza** for dinner, but you really wanted CHINESE FOOD. What do you do?

a. You don't say anything.

b. Agree to get pizza tonight, if you can order Chinese next time.

c. SCREAM, refuse to eat, and leave the room.

4. Your sister took your *favorite sweater* — again. What do you do?

a. Nothing. Even though it's your favorite sweater, and she **ruined** another sweater of yours.

b. Tell her she can borrow the **pink t-shirt** she likes, but not your sweater.

c. SCREAM at her and steal all of her sweaters.

If you scored:

MOSTLY A'S: Talk to your siblings! They won't know how you feel unless you tell them — using words.

MOSTLY B'S: You're doing a good job communicating with your siblings. Keep it up!

MOSTLY C'S: You're letting anger get the best of you. Try calming down and explaining how you feel.

FIGHTING WITH A SIBLING

Sometimes Jimmy and I fight. We usually *resolve* the problem quickly, but not always. Here's how to **fix a fight** with a sibling.

Step One: Identify the problem.

Step Two: Tell your stories. Give each person time to talk.

Step Three: Work it out. Find a solution that makes both people happy. If you can't, start over with step one, or ask a parent for help.

DON'T:

Talk about other fights. If Jimmy's mad because he thinks I took his shirt, he shouldn't bring up the time I borrowed his skateboard. That's **not fair fighting**.

I AM A T-SHIRT

Call names. It's just common sense. **Name-calling** just makes people madder, and it doesn't help solve the fight.

Get other people involved (unless they're your parents). Dragging your friends into the fight isn't cool.

Let the fight go on too long. Try to solve it fast. But that doesn't mean you can't take a break sometimes. Cooling off might help both of you.

Yell. Keep your voice calm, and you'll both feel calmer.

Get violent. That's just asking for more trouble.

ASK FOR HELP FROM A PARENT WHEN YOU NEED IT. If the fight can't be resolved, you need outside help to fix the problem.

LISTEN. Give the other person your full attention when they're speaking. That way you can expect the same from them.

TRY TO STAY CALM. If not, it might make things worse.

KEEP WORKING. Make solving the fight your goal, and it'll happen!

▷ CHAPTER 4
BRANCHING OUT:
Who else lives in your family tree

Did you ever have to do a **family tree project** for school? Think about what it looked like. Your name, along with your parents' and siblings' names, was near the center.

Your grandparents' names probably came next. They were farther out on the *branches*. Then aunts and uncles, and then cousins.

Branches are an important part of a tree. And your grandparents, aunts, uncles, and cousins make up an important part of your family.

Grandparents love SPOILING you. They are fun to hang out with. And they usually have the best stories. Aunts and uncles are good at spoiling, too. Cousins are sort of like extra siblings.

Here is a look at my family tree. *How does it compare to yours?*

My family tree

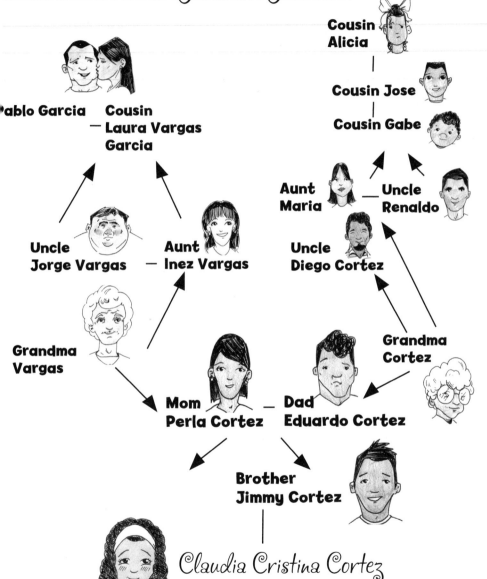

Cousin Alicia

Cousin Jose

Cousin Gabe

Pablo Garcia

Cousin Laura Vargas Garcia

Aunt Maria

Uncle Renaldo

Uncle Jorge Vargas

Aunt Inez Vargas

Uncle Diego Cortez

Grandma Vargas

Grandma Cortez

Mom Perla Cortez

Dad Eduardo Cortez

Brother Jimmy Cortez

Claudia Cristina Cortez

COPING WITH COUSINS

I don't have very many COUSINS. There are three younger ones on my dad's side of the family, and one older one on my mom's side.

Cousins can be kind of difficult to deal with. In my family, my aunts and uncles and parents *expect us to get along*, even if we don't like each other. They think since they like each other, their kids will like each other too. They expect us to do things together, even if we don't want to.

When my family traveled to Florida for my great-grandpa's birthday celebration, I thought it was going to be a **fun vacation**. Until I got there.

That's when I realized that I was going to be stuck watching my **BRATTY COUSINS**, Alisha, Jose, and Gabe. I was not happy about that!

I wanted to have fun. I wanted to swim in the ocean. I wanted to hang out with the friends I met in Florida. But instead I had to spend time with my cousins. Gabe cried all the time. Jose just wanted to watch TV. And Alisha **acted like a brat**.

Every spare second I had, somebody made me watch my cousins.

It was NOT FUN.

By the end of the trip, though, I started to like them.

Jose and Gabe were just acting like little kids. They were having just as bad of a time as I was. So I took them to a *Pirate Parade*. They got to catch candy and jewelry, and they loved it!

And Alisha was just JEALOUS of me! It turned out that she had a crush on my friend Mason. She also felt jealous because I was older than her. So I gave her a **MAKEOVER** and explained that Mason was just my friend. And after that, Alisha relaxed. We had a nice time together.

My older cousin on my mom's side of the family is named Laura.

When I was younger, Laura was like a big sister to me. Whenever we got together, she and I would *stay up late*. We watched movies, talked, and listened to music.

So I was really excited when Laura asked me to be a *junior bridesmaid* in her wedding. But when my mom and I arrived at Laura's house a few days before the wedding, I started feeling bad.

Laura didn't seem to care that I was there. I felt like I was getting in her way and annoying her. (Just like my little cousins had annoyed me in Florida.) I felt like Laura was growing up and **leaving me way behind.**

Luckily, I realized that wasn't true. She was just busy with her wedding. She was growing up, but she wasn't leaving me anywhere.

In fact, at her wedding, she gave me a *special bracelet* that had belonged to our grandmother. And after the wedding, she invited me to come and stay with her and her new husband at their new house.

I guess the LESSON I LEARNED is that cousins are people too. You might not always like them, but they usually don't mean any harm.

OTHER FAMILY MEMBERS (and what they're best at — at least in my family)

‹‹

AUNTS: Good for confiding in, going shopping, seeing *chick flicks*, giving book recommendations, cooking meals together

UNCLES: Good for playing Frisbee, **telling jokes**, watching funny movies, sneaking extra helpings of dessert

GREAT-GRANDPARENTS: Good for hearing stories about the past, watching serious movies, **talking about books**

DISTANT RELATIVES: Good for hearing funny stories about your parents, **LEARNING** about other parts of the country or world

NEPHEWS/NIECES: I don't have any of these (yet) but it would be really fun to have a baby in the family. Maybe in a few years, Jimmy will get married and have kids. Then I'll be *Aunt Claudia!*

GRANDPARENTS ARE GREAT!

Grandparents are a *link to the past.* You probably don't know your great-grandparents. (If you do, you're really lucky!) So grandparents are a great way to find out more about your family's history.

I like to spend a lot of time with my grandma. She comes over to my house a lot, since she lives nearby.

I've noticed that she gets away with more than I can get away with. For example, when we went on vacation, my dad said we could each bring only **one suitcase**. Grandma got to bring two.

Everyone else had to be ready right away in the morning. Grandma took her time.

If I said I had to go to the bathroom, Dad said I could hold it for a while. If Grandma said she did, Dad would STOP the car **RIGHT AWAY**.

I didn't think that was fair. But then I remembered that Grandma is Dad's mom. He has to do what she says!

I guess it's only fair that grandmas should get away with more than kids do. After all, they are older and *wiser*.

Grandma is really fun to be with. She and I both like **big words** and board games, pancakes, peanut butter and strawberry jam sandwiches, and *swimming*.

She lets me listen to my **BIG DOG** CDs (Dad thinks their music is terrible).

When she stays at our house, she bakes cookies while I'm at school. Then I have a great treat when I get home.

But I don't like to talk about everything with her. For example, I don't really like talking about LOVE STUFF with Grandma. I know she'd give me good advice, but it's *awkward* to talk about boys with her. After all, she hasn't dated anyone for, like, sixty years!

Things are different now. And not just dating. Think about the ways the world is different now from when your grandparents were your age.

THINGS THAT ARE DIFFERENT:

- *Everything* costs more

- More women have jobs

- The country is more **diverse**

- You can now buy things, talk to people, and get all kinds of information without ever leaving your house

- When my grandma was my age, no African-American people had ever been **PRESIDENT OF THE UNITED STATES**

- Alaska and Hawaii weren't even states

Things that have been invented since my grandma was my age: The Internet, **CELL PHONES**, DVDs, hybrid cars, computers, cordless phones, digital watches, video games, CDs, microwaves, microwave popcorn, HARRY POTTER, color TV, MTV, cable, Sesame Street, the Simpsons, Starbucks, McDonalds, Coldstone Creamery, the chicken pox vaccine

Talk to your grandparents about what life was like when they were your age. You might be **SURPRISED** to hear about ways in which their lives were like yours!

QUESTIONS FOR GRANDPARENTS

- How did you meet your wife or husband?

- What were your parents like?

- What was your **favorite class** in school?

- Where did you live?

- What was your house like?

- What did you do to *help out* around the house?

- What was your first job?

- Did you have any PETS when you grew up?

- What are some **HISTORICAL EVENTS** that you remember?

Write down their answers, and save them **somewhere special**. Someday, you can read the responses to your own grandchildren, and fill in answers of your own.

▷ CHAPTER 5
HOME LIFE:
How to enjoy family time, meals, & even chores

You probably spend most of your ⅁⅍⅊ⅈℒⅆ ⅏ⅈℳⅇ at home. Most people do. And everyone's home is different. It all depends on the family. (Like we already discussed, all families are different).

When you spend a lot of time at home with your family, you might feel:

- **bored**
- *lonely*
- STUCK IN A RUT

That's because most families are pretty **predictable**. That's a good thing. It's nice to know that dinner will always be at 6, your mom will always watch the news at 10, and your brother will always play video games as soon as he's done clearing the table. But sometimes that gets boring.

It doesn't have to be like that. *Family time can be fun time too!*

(UNEXPECTED) FAMILY FUN

It was **Saturday night.** I didn't have any plans.

I called Monica. She had a cold.

I called **Becca**. She was at her grandma's house.

I called **ADAM**. He was at a baseball game with his dad.

I called TOMMY. No one answered the phone at his house.

I called **Peter**. He was busy studying.

I had to face facts. I wasn't going to do anything with my friends that night.

Everybody knows that being **STUCK AT HOME** on a Saturday night might be the **worst night ever.** But it doesn't have to be.

If you're in that situation, have no fear: You can actually make it a FUN NIGHT! Try one of the tricks on the next few pages.

Laugh, play, and (maybe) win! As long as there are **no sore losers** (or mean winners) in your family, a game night is an awesome way to spend time together.

Skip dinner and have *finger-food* snacks instead. Try egg rolls, mini pizzas, nuts, cut-up fruit and veggies, or whatever your family's favorites are.

Have prizes for winners. They could get a day off from chores, an **extra scoop** of ice cream at dessert, their favorite meal for dinner, etc. Think up your own!

SOME GAMES THAT YOU CAN PLAY:

- Board games

- Jigsaw puzzles

- Split into teams for Wheel of Fortune or Trivial Pursuit. Or play "family pursuit," and make up your own trivia about your family

- Video games, if there's an option for more than one player

MOVIE NIGHT

Curl up together in front of a couple of movies. Try having themes, like *Action Night,* or Adam Sandler Night, or Movies About Dogs Night. Or take turns letting one person pick out the movies. **Pop popcorn** and enjoy!

TRY THESE TOPPINGS ON YOUR POPCORN:

• Butter

• Cheese powder or **parmesan cheese**

• GARLIC SALT and a little olive oil

• A few spoonfuls of powdered ranch dressing mix

• Instant **hot cocoa powder** and a little melted butter for chocolaty popcorn

• Mix with M&MS or other small chocolate candy

• Taco seasoning

• For **CLASSIC KETTLE CORN**, mix plain air-popped popcorn with oil, salt, and sugar

FAMILY OLYMPICS

In my family, sometimes we do the **Cortez Olympics.** It's a fun way to be active and enjoy spending time together. **Here are some of the events we have:**

- Best SOMERSAULT
- Most **Jumping Jacks** in One Minute
- Macaroni and Cheese *Eating Contest*
- Biggest **Leap**
- **STARING** Contest
- Tallest Ice Cream Sundae

The person who wins each event gets a special ribbon. At the end of the night, the person with the most ribbons wins the GRAND PRIZE. My mom usually picks out the grand prize. Sometimes it's money or your favorite meal. Sometimes it's a **weekend without chores!**

VOLUNTEERING

As a family, CHOOSE A CAUSE you feel is really important. Then spend time volunteering.

HERE ARE SOME IDEAS TO GET YOU STARTED:

- **Homeless shelters** — Serve meals
- *Animal shelters* — Walk dogs, play with cats
- **Habitat for Humanity** — Help build a home for a local family
- *Local food shelves* — Collect canned or boxed food
- **Church or school events** — Support local churches or schools
- *Libraries* — Read books to kids or dust book shelves

Volunteering is **A GREAT WAY TO SPEND TIME WITH YOUR FAMILY** and feel good about helping other people.

SCRAPBOOK NIGHT

Create family memories together. Buy blank scrapbooks. Then fill them a page at a time with family photos and other *keepsakes*.

TRY MAKING PAGES ABOUT:

- Holidays

- Birthdays

- Graduations

- Weddings

- Vacations

- School or work events

- Pets

Use STICKERS, cut out pictures and words from **MAGAZINES**, or buy special scrapbooking materials. Every person should use his or her *own style* to make their scrapbook page PERFECT!

BACKYARD CAMPING

Set up a tent in your backyard. Bring sleeping bags and pillows. ROAST MARSHMALLOWS and hot dogs. Drink hot cocoa. You don't have to go out of town or even get in the car to enjoy a night of **CAMPING OUT** with your family!

For the **perfect backyard campout**, try:

- Telling *ghost stories*
- Looking at the STARS and making up names for constellations
- Building a **campfire** (make sure there are parents present, of course!)
- **Singing favorite songs**
- Reading using **flashlights**
- **Playing cards** around a lantern

FAMILY MEALS

Let's say you eat dinner with your family every night. And let's say each meal lasts for 20 minutes. That's **more than 120 hours spent with your family** at the dinner table every year. That's a long time! It's as much time as if you spent five days in a row at the dinner table.

My family doesn't have time to eat together every night. Sometimes I eat at a friend's house. Sometimes Jimmy is at band practice. Sometimes my dad is TOO BUSY AT WORK to make it home in time for dinner. But I like it best when all four of us are there.

Sometimes other people are at our house for dinner, like Grandma, Uncle Diego, or one of my friends. That's fun too.

No matter what, we try to make sure *dinnertime is fun, easygoing, and drama-free.*

Sometimes it's hard to think of things to talk about at the dinner table. It is especially **bad** if you're really TIRED or you had a *bad day*. But dinner is more fun when people talk. Here are some ideas to make dinnertime talk flow:

- Ask the person sitting at your left a *question*. Go around the table until everyone has been asked a question.

- Go around the table and **list one good and one bad thing** that happened that day.

- Talk about something new you learned that day. Ask others to think of something new they learned. You might be surprised!

- Plan a **family vacation** or special day.

- Ask your parents to tell you about what dinnertime was like when they were growing up.

- Tell jokes. Before dinner, ask everyone to prepare their **FAVORITE, FUNNIEST JOKE**. Whichever joke gets the most laughs, wins!

FAMILY FOOD FEUD

My dad's favorite meal is **SPAGHETTI WITH MEATBALLS.**
My mom really likes having FISH.

My brother loves **pizza**. I go crazy for macaroni
and cheese. But Jimmy HATES fish. My mom doesn't
eat red meat. And my dad can't have cheese because
it makes him **SICK!**

When we go out to dinner, I usually want to
get **hamburgers**. Mom always chooses Italian
food. Jimmy refuses to go anywhere that doesn't
serve steak. And Dad always wants **CHINESE FOOD.**
It's hard for us to ever agree.

Food is the cause of many arguments for some
families (including mine). To deal with that, we trade
off deciding what we'll eat each night. And if we
go out to dinner, we *draw straws* to see who will
choose where we go.

Meals don't have to be **stressful**. They can
be a time for families to enjoy each other — and
some GOOD FOOD!

FUN FOR FOODIES

Usually, parents are in charge of meals. But **KIDS CAN COOK** too! Treat your family to a meal. To make it a really special occasion, try some of these tricks:

- Ask your guests to **dress up** for the meal.

- Make *place cards* so everyone knows where to sit.

- Use **CLOTH NAPKINS** and pretend you're in a **FANCY** restaurant.

- Create a few options for each course and make *menus* so that everyone can choose their meal.

- Don't forget **DESSERT!**

The meals on the next few pages are just ideas. You can change them to match your family's likes and dislikes, favorites, and traditions.

Bon appetit! (That's French for "Enjoy the meal!")

BIRTHDAY BASH

Appetizer: Veggie cups. Slice the top off of a green pepper. Use a spoon to clean out the inside of the pepper. Then put a little of your favorite dip or salsa in the bottom of the pepper. Fill the pepper with carrot and celery sticks.

Main course: Pizza. Top store-bought dough with the birthday person's favorite toppings. Or split the pizza up and make a section with each person's favorites. Bake as directed.

Dessert: Birthday cake, of course! Buy a plain, unfrosted angel food cake at the grocery store. Frost it with premade frosting and add sprinkles, chocolate chips, or other candies. Don't forget the candles!

Beverage: Red-Letter-Day Sparkler. Mix equal parts cranberry juice and seltzer. Add a squeeze of lime juice. Pour over ice. Serve right away, with a wedge of lime on the rim of the glass.

V *Appetizer:* Green salad. Mix together:

1 BAG OF PRE-WASHED LETTUCE

1 TOMATO, CUT UP

1 CUCUMBER, SLICED

Let each person top their salad with croutons, cheese, and their favorite dressing.

Main Course: Peanut butter and jelly sandwiches. To make it extra special, let each person choose their favorite kind of bread and jelly. Have a few options to pick from.

Dessert: Ice cream sundae bar. Serve each person a dish of vanilla ice cream. Then let them add their own toppings. Some ideas: different kinds of sauce (hot fudge, cherry, caramel), candy (crushed candy bars, cinnamon candies, chocolate chips), sprinkles, cherries, and whipped cream.

Beverage: Sparkling apple juice. Buy a bottle, or mix regular apple juice with seltzer.

Appetizer: Tomato soup. Heat up soup from a can, and make it special by sprinkling a little dried basil on top.

Main course: Grilled cheese sandwiches. Butter one side of two pieces of bread. Put them into a hot pan, butter side down, on the stove. Top each piece with a slice of American cheese. When the bottoms are toasted, put the pieces together. After about a minute, flip the sandwich.

(You can also try making it in the microwave: toast two slices of bread, then layer with cheese and put in the microwave for 45 seconds.)

Dessert and beverage in one: Mint hot chocolate. Make hot chocolate as directed on the package. Add a small drop of peppermint extract to each mug. Top with whipped cream and red sprinkles.

Appetizer: Cold gazpacho. Gazpacho is a Spanish soup. Cut into small pieces and mix together in a bowl: 4 tomatoes, ½ small onion, 1 cucumber, 1 green pepper, and a handful of fresh cilantro. Stir together with ½ cup tomato juice, 1/8th tsp salt, 1/8th tsp pepper, 2 tsp olive oil, and 1 tsp vinegar. Serve cold. Add hot sauce for an extra kick.

Main course: Veggie wraps. For each wrap, spread one flour tortilla with cream cheese. Add slices of tomato, chopped lettuce, chopped onion, and avocado. Roll up and serve.

Dessert: Fruit kabobs. You'll need a watermelon, a cantaloupe, a bunch of grapes, and some strawberries. Cut the watermelon and cantaloupe into bite-sized pieces. Stick all of the fruit onto long wooden skewers.

Beverage: Lemonade. Buy it pre-made. Or make it yourself by squeezing lemons into a pitcher and adding sugar and water.

McLean County Unit #5
201-EJHS

CHIP IN WITH CHORES

In my family, **chores aren't an option**. They're something you have to do because you're a member of the family.

But that doesn't mean I like doing them.

Still, *I don't argue* when my mom asks me to help with the laundry or the dishes (most of the time, anyway). The FASTER I can get them done, the more time I have to spend doing things I want to do.

If I can **WASH THE DISHES** in ten minutes instead of fifteen, that's five more minutes I can spend chatting with Becca.

If I get the laundry into the washing machine in five minutes instead of ten, that's five more minutes I can spend *listening to music* in my room.

If I can set the table in two minutes instead of five, that's three extra minutes to **read my book** before dinner.

What about you? **If you had more time, what would you use it for?**

What kind of chores do you have to do?

Laundry: Wash, fold, put away = 2 hours

Dishes: Wash, dry, put away = 20 minutes

Dishwasher: Rinse, load, unload = 5 minutes each

Vacuum floors = 10 minutes each

Sweep floors = 10 minutes each

Setting & clearing the table = 5 minutes each

Bathroom: Clean floor, clean sink, clean tub, clean toilet = 40 minutes

Take out garbage = 5 minutes

Walk dog = 20 minutes

Scoop cat's litter box = 5 minutes

Feed pet = 3 minutes

How can you make those chores go faster? If you're like me, *you'll find a way!*

ALLOWANCE?

In some families, the kids get allowances. That means their *parents give them money* every week (or every month).

I don't get an allowance. Neither does Jimmy. But we still **have to help out** around the house.

Monica gets an allowance of $10 every week. Her little sister gets $5. When I first found out, I was JEALOUS and MAD. I didn't think it was fair that Monica got money from her parents for **doing nothing**.

But it's my job to help my mom with the laundry. I also have to do the dishes when I'm home for dinner.

Jimmy has to mow the lawn and shovel snow. He also has to vacuum the living room once a week. I'm just glad I don't have to clean the bathroom. GROSS!

Dad says that's what we have to do as members of the family. **Everyone needs to chip in**, since everyone lives in the house and eats the food.

(Of course, I know they'd take care of us even if we didn't do chores. But then I'd be grounded for life. **I'd rather do chores than be grounded.**)

But that doesn't mean I never have any money. I do chores and run errands for my neighbors to *make money*.

I save most of it to buy a car. But sometimes I use a little of my savings to buy something I've been wanting for **a long time**. I might buy a new shirt or download a new album by my favorite band, **BAD DOG.**

My parents help me save money. When I was ten, my dad took me to the bank. He helped me open up my own **savings account**.

Now, I keep cash in my room. When I've saved $50, I keep $10 and go to the bank to deposit the rest. Dad thinks that's the best way to **keep saving**.

When I'm sixteen, I hope I'll have enough money saved up to BUY A CAR right away! (It might take me a few more years.)

MAKE CHORES FUN

Chores aren't fun. (That's why they're called "chores" and not "fun times".) But they don't have to be totally boring. With a little bit of *imagination*, you can make doing your chores a fun part of your life.

HERE ARE SOME IDEAS!

- Set a **TIMER** for five minutes and see how many things you can pick up in your bedroom.

- Have **BED–MAKING CONTESTS** with your siblings.

- Play *rock-paper-scissors* for different chores or parts of a chore.

- **Hold Cleaning Olympics.** Everyone in the family can participate and make chores a little more fun. Ask a parent to judge. Who sweeps the floor better? Who cleans the sink better? Who washes the dishes better? *Whoever takes home the most gold medals wins!*

What if you really *hate your chores?* Try trading with a sibling.

Once I was so sick of helping with the laundry that I decided to try to get out of it. I offered to shovel the sidewalk for Jimmy if he'd fold the laundry for me. It turned out that he was **really sick of shoveling snow**, so he was glad to trade.

Or talk to your parents about giving you a different chore for a while.

Maybe you could even make up a CHORE CALENDAR that would rotate, so you'd never get stuck with the same chore for long.

I bet that your parents will be so glad that you want to keep helping out around the house that they'll be happy to figure out a way to make it *less boring* for you!

Like I said, chores aren't fun. But they are **A FACT OF MIDDLE SCHOOL LIFE**, at least in my house.

▷CHAPTER 6
FAMILY FUN:
Making the most of vacations & holidays

When my family drove to Florida on vacation, there were a lot of us PACKED into the car. There was my dad, my mom, Uncle Diego, Grandma, Jimmy, and me.

Dad drove. Uncle Diego mostly slept. Grandma complained. Mom read. Jimmy played video games. And *I felt bored.*

Next time, I'm going to be prepared. **Here's what I will bring.**

- **SNACKS.** Nothing too salty or sweet. Nothing that makes STINKY garbage. I like mixes of dried fruits and nuts, or granola bars. Don't forget a bottle of water.

- A **BOOK** or **MAGAZINES**

- **MUSIC.** If your family can't agree on music, bring your own headphones.

- A book of **WORD OR NUMBER PUZZLES**

- A **SKETCHBOOK** and pen or pencil

- A **NOTEBOOK** for writing

- **VIDEO GAMES** and extra batteries

- A digital **CAMERA**

For fun, Grandma and I did *play games*. Here are some fun things for your car crew to do on a long trip:

License plate bingo: Before you leave, make **BINGO CARDS**. Draw three lines down a sheet of paper and three lines across it. Fill in the sixteen boxes with names of different states. Make at least **one card for each player**. Make sure that all the states are different and are in different places on the sheets. To play as you're driving, *look at the license plates* of other cars. When you see a license plate from one of the states on your bingo card, make an X through it. The first person to get four in a row wins. (Then trade cards and play again!)

Alphabet game: This is a great game when there are little kids in the car. Starting with the letter A, everyone has to look out the window and find the **WHOLE ALPHABET**. Look for letters on billboards, road signs, and other cars (but license plates don't count!). You can do it as a group or separately. I think the hardest letter to find is Z. I hope you'll pass a **ZOO!**

I Spy: One person picks an object, person, plant, or animal, and the other players have to guess what it is. My brother Jimmy is the **BEST** at this game. I can never guess his objects! Once we played and he was thinking of a **buttonhole**. It took my whole family three hours to solve that one. **We almost gave up!**

Book on CD: On some road trips, my family and I pick out a book on CD from the library. This is especially good when you're driving at night, because there's not much to look at.

FAMILY INTERVIEWS

Whether you're on vacation or at home, spending time with your family is a **great opportunity** to learn more about the people you're related to.

Take turns asking each other questions. By the end of the trip, you'll know a lot more about each other.

Sample questions can be:

- What's your FAVORITE TV SHOW?

- What do you want to be when you **grow up**? (Or, when you were my age, what did you want to be when you grew up?)

- What's the *best thing* that happened to you this year?

- What's your favorite ANIMAL?

- Do you prefer **sweet** or SALTY food?

- If you could go anywhere on vacation, **WHERE WOULD YOU GO?**

During holidays, lots of families get together in big groups. It can be really fun to see everyone, but it can be *stressful*, too.

Relatives you hardly know **pinch your cheeks** and ask you if you have a boyfriend.

There are lots of good things to eat, but you end up OVEREATING and never want to see another cookie.

You're STUCK in the car with your family while you drive to and from holiday events.

You get presents, but then you have to write thank-you notes.

It's fun to tell your friends about presents you got, but if there's **A POPULAR SNOB** at your school like there is at mine, she got bigger and better presents and wants you to feel bad about it (even though you liked your presents).

Holidays are fun, but they don't come very often. *Maybe that's a good thing!*

Many holidays come with the *tradition* of gift-giving. Stumped about what to give someone? Try one of these ideas.

A good gift for _____ is _____

MOM	Something you made
DAD	A nice photo in a frame
GRANDMA	Pretty stationery
GRANDPA	A book about something he's interested in
OLDER SIBLING	Coupons that they can give you and you'll do their chores for a day
YOUNGER SIBLING	Trip to the toy store or park
COUSIN	Movie tickets
AUNT/UNCLE	Gift card to a restaurant, book store, or sports event

FAMILY TRADITIONS

Holidays are the perfect time to take part in family traditions. *I love traditions.* They give me something to look forward to at each holiday. Plus, some of my best memories are family traditions.

Here are a few of the traditions we do on some of my favorite holidays.

New Year's Eve

My parents, Jimmy, and I always go out for LUNCH on New Year's Eve. Then we go **shopping** to pick up noisemakers and snacks for later that night. We spend the evening playing games. Then we watch the BALL DROP on TV.

Saint Patrick's Day

We aren't Irish. But Dad says EVERYONE IS IRISH on Saint Patrick's Day. Every year, Mom, Jimmy, and I plan a special dinner. The rule is that **everything has to be green!** Shamrock shake, anyone?

Summer Solstice

I know, I know. It isn't really a holiday. But my family has some great traditions for the **first day of summer.** Every year, we have a campout in our backyard. We roast hot dogs and marshmallows over a fire. Then we play GHOSTS IN THE GRAVEYARD.

Fourth of July

On this holiday we go to the local **Patriot Parade**. My grandma — and any other family who happens to be in town — comes with us too. After the parade we head to a park. There are great games to play and great food to eat. After cheering on our favorite players at a baseball game, we all watch FIREWORKS.

Thanksgiving

It isn't hard to figure out our Thanksgiving traditions. They include **A BIG DINNER** with turkey, mashed potatoes, cranberries, and pie. Grandma makes her famous TAMALES too. I look forward to them all year! After we eat, we watch a little football on TV. Then we head outside for a game of our own.

P.S.

SOME OF THE THINGS I BELIEVE ABOUT FAMILIES:

○ All families are DIFFERENT. There are as many kinds of families as there are kinds of people.

○ **Your family knows you better than anyone,** even when you feel like they don't understand you at all.

○ *Family is fun!*

○ You should be able to **count on the people in your family**. And they should be able to count on you.

○ Having a **big brother** is actually pretty cool.

o Grandparents tell the *best stories*.

o Being with your family is the best way to CELEBRATE a holiday or a special occasion.

o **FAMILIES ARE INTERESTING.**

o Being with your family can be BORING sometimes. *That's okay*.

o Moms love to **listen**.

o Dads LOVE hearing about your day.

o If you need help, you should be able to find it in your family.

I love my family!

ABOUT THE AUTHOR

Diana G. Gallagher lives in Florida with her husband and five dogs, four cats, and a CRANKY parrot. Her hobbies are gardening, garage sales, and grandchildren. She has been an English equitation instructor, a professional folk musician, and an artist. However, she had aspirations to be a professional writer at the age of twelve. She has written *dozens of books* for kids and young adults.

ABOUT THE ILLUSTRATOR

Brann Garvey lives in Minneapolis, Minnesota with his wife, Keegan, their dog, Lola, and their very fat cat, Iggy. Brann graduated from Iowa State University with **A BACHELOR OF FINE ARTS DEGREE.** He later attended the Minneapolis College of Art and Design, where he studied illustration. In his free time, Brann enjoys being with his family and friends. *He brings his sketchbook everywhere he goes.*

GLOSSARY

annoy (uh-NOI)—to make someone lose patience or feel angry

awkward (AWK-wurd)—difficult or uncomfortable

communicating (kuh-MYOO-nuh-kate-ing)—sharing feelings with another person by talking or writing

embarrass (em-BARE-uhss)—to give a feeling of discomfort

fester (FES-tur)—to grow increasingly worse

mortifying (MORT-uh-fye-ing)—something very embarrassing; causing extreme discomfort

predictable (pri-DIK-tuh-buhl)—easily able to say what will happen in the future

resolve (ri-ZOLV)—to fix a problem

volunteering (vol-uhn-TEER-ing)—doing a job or service without pay

 DISCUSSION QUESTIONS

1. Describe your *family*. What is your family's greatest strength?

2. Claudia and her friends swapped stories about how their parents **embarrass** them. How do your parents embarrass you? How do you handle it?

3. If you could change ONE THING about your siblings, what would you change? Why?

WRITING ACTIVITY

Pretend you are an **ADVICE COLUMNIST** for your favorite
magazine. What advice would you give to solve these
problems?

1. My parents have the EXACT SAME RULES for
   me and my little brother. The problem is he's eight
   and I'm thirteen! How can I get them to loosen up?

2. My older sister and I used to be great friends, but
   since she started **high school**, all she does is sit
   in her room, talking on the phone to all her high
   school friends. *I miss her*. How can I get her to
   like me again?

3. My parents expect me to be **THE GREATEST KID
   IN THE UNIVERSE.** They expect me to be my
   grade's top student, the captain of the basketball
   team, first-chair trumpet in band, and the lead
   in the school play. **THE PRESSURE IS GETTING TO ME!**
   What do I do?

STRAIGHT FROM TEENS

Here's what real teens, just like you, have to say about dealing with family.

If you can't talk to your parents or siblings about something in person, then let all of your feelings out through a note. You can express yourself better. They will see your side more clearly. Don't hold back. They need to know what you are feeling.

—*Shelby, 17*

If your parents are always unfair and don't seem to trust you, then you should sit down with them and tell them how you feel about it. If you let them know how you really feel, they may choose to give you more chances to prove to them they can trust you.

—*Kelli, 16*

READ UP
FOR MORE GREAT ADVICE!

☆ *For Girls Only: Wise Words, Good Advice*
by Carol Weston

☆ *How to Raise Your Parents: A Teen Girl's Survival Guide*
by Sarah O'Leary Burningham

☆ *Life Lists for Teens: Tips, Steps, Hints, and How-tos for Growing Up, Getting Along, Learning, and Having Fun* by Pamela Espeland

☆ *Stepliving for Teens: Getting Along with Stepparents, Parents, and Siblings* by Joel D. Block and Susan S. Bartell

☆ *Yes, Your Parents are Crazy! A Teen Survival Guide* by Michael J. Bradley

CLAUDIA
CRISTINA CORTEZ

MORE FUN
with Claudia!

When you're thirteen, like Claudia, life is complicated. Luckily, Claudia has lots of ways to cope with family, friends, school, work, and play. And she's sharing her advice with you! Read all of Claudia's advice books and uncomplicate your life.

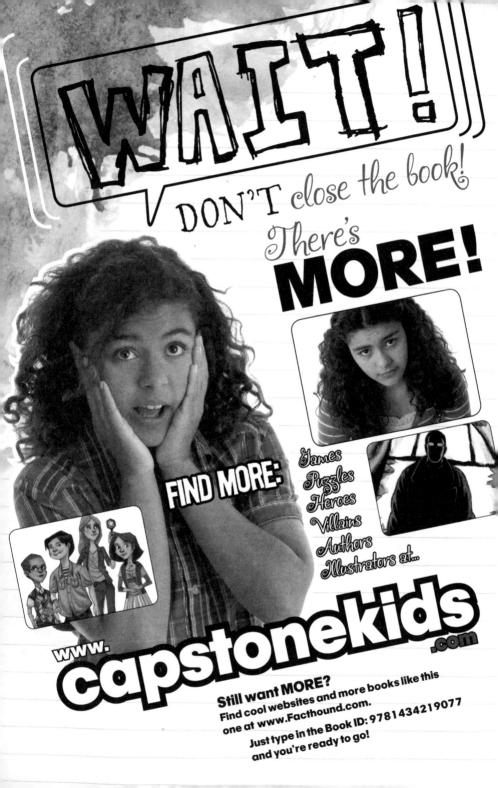